DATE			

The Shell Woman & the King

The Shell Woman & the King

A Chinese Folktale retold by **Laurence Yep**

paintings by **Yang Ming-Yi**

DIAL BOOKS FOR YOUNG READERS  NEW YORK

This folktale comes from an eighteenth-century collection of Chinese tales. The original tale does not explain why Uncle Wu married the shell woman, so I've tried to answer that question. At the same time, I've set the tale in the kingdom of the Southern Han (917–971 A.D.), whose kings were fabled for their extravagance as well as for their cruelty.
L.Y.

Published by Dial Books for Young Readers
A Division of Penguin Books USA Inc.
375 Hudson Street
New York, New York 10014

Designed by Amelia Lau Carling
Printed in Hong Kong
by South China Printing Company (1988) Limited
First Edition
1 3 5 7 9 10 8 6 4 2

Library of Congress Cataloging in Publication Data
Yep, Laurence.
The shell woman & the king / by Laurence Yep ;
paintings by Yang Ming-Yi.
p. cm.
Summary: To save herself and her husband from an evil king, Shell agrees to bring him three wonders.
ISBN 0-8037-1394-0 (tr); ISBN 0-8037-1395-9 (lib. bdg.)
[1. Fairy tales. 2. Folklore—China.]
I. Yang, Ming-Yi, ill. II. Title.
PZ8.Y46Sh 1993 398.2—dc20 [E] 92-9583 CIP AC

The art for each picture consists of an ink and watercolor painting, which is scanner-separated and reproduced in full color. The colored pattern behind the type is reproduced from a special silk used for mounting scrolls.

To Phyllis Look,
who makes the impossible happen
L.Y.

To my wife
Y.M.Y.

Long ago in a kingdom in southern China there was a good man called Uncle Wu whom everyone liked and who liked everyone. He was fond of saying that he had only loved once, but the girl had married someone else.

When he felt especially lonely, he would go down to the beach where he would sing love songs to the restless sea. One day when he had finished singing, he heard a girl's voice.

Now, this king lived in a splendid palace. Its wooden walls were inlaid with silver. Its left tower was decorated with amber. During the day it gleamed with a golden light so brilliant that the king named it his tower of the sun. The right tower was decorated with shining crystal. At night it glistened with a light so cold and white that the king called it his tower of the moon. Morning or evening his palace shone so bright that it almost blinded anyone who tried to gaze upon it.

Word eventually reached the ears of one of the king's spies, and he went immediately to the cruel ruler of that land.

"Not only is she beautiful," the spy informed the king, "but she can change herself into a shell, so that is her name."

Often they would return to the ocean, where Shell would change herself into her sea form. Then she would fetch all sorts of delicacies from the gardens of the sea. Other times she would bring back curiosities such as the wool from water sheep. Uncle Wu was proud of his talented wife, and he liked to brag about her to their village.

Before his eyes she changed herself into a large seashell.

After she had resumed her human shape, Uncle Wu looked at her sadly. "I'm afraid I don't have your talents. I can't change myself into anything. Do you mind?"

"Not at all," Shell said, laughing. And so they were married.

"It's a shame to waste so much love on cold, empty waves," she said.

Turning, Uncle Wu saw a beautiful girl in a robe of pink and yellow. He was terribly embarrassed. "Now you know my secret."

The girl promised never to tell and introduced herself as Shell. An orphan, she lived in a little reed hut she had built among the sand dunes.

After that meeting Uncle Wu visited Shell often to chat. She was so bright and sweet that soon Uncle Wu realized he had come to love her. However, when he asked her to marry him, she hesitated.

"I have a secret too," she said. "I am from the sea. But when I first heard you singing, I was curious to meet you."

Within his palace the king kept all sorts of wonders: A parrot who could recite all the classics. Hairs from the tail of a unicorn. A dragon's egg. But as magnificent as his palace was, this evil ruler was not happy.

"A matchless sovereign with a matchless palace must have a matchless queen," the king declared, and sent his soldiers to bring back Shell and her husband.

After he ordered his guards to take Uncle Wu to the dungeon, he commanded Shell to do her magic for him. So Shell changed herself into her sea form and then became human again. The king could not take his eyes from her. "Leave your husband and become my queen," he said.

Shell stared back at him. "I won't. I love my husband," she answered.

The king became angry. "Then you must give me three wonders in your place. Or I will cut off your husband's head and hang it from one of my towers, and you will become my queen anyway."

Shell had no choice but to agree, and the king smiled evilly.

"First, I want the hair from a toad," he said.

Shell nodded and left the castle. She returned the next evening carrying a plain bowl.

The king looked inside the bowl. "There's nothing in here. What kind of fool do you take me for?" he shouted. And he threw it down in disgust.

"A toad's hair is so fine that it's invisible," Shell explained. "I trimmed it from the toad in the moon. He will shiver tonight until he can grow a new coat tomorrow. And the moon will shake with him."

And sure enough, when the king looked out the windows of the throne room, he saw the moon rocking back and forth in the sky.

The king wanted her even more now that he had seen how really magical she was. "Not far from here is a hill covered with flowers. In that hill is a ghost. Bring me the arm of that ghost."

Shell wasn't the least bit dismayed. "May I use your kitchen?" she asked.

Puzzled, the king gave her the run of the kitchen, where Shell began to make dumplings and other snacks.

Then she packed them all up in a basket with an old knife, and she went out to the hill covered with fragrant white jasmine like a mound of stars.

Setting out her picnic, she waited as her shadow swung back and forth under the quivering moon. Suddenly an arm snaked out of the dirt and began to reach for the plate of snacks. Snatching the knife from the basket, Shell cut the arm off.

There was a terrifying shriek and the mound trembled, but Shell calmly packed up the arm and the knife and the rest of the meal and put them all into the basket.

That morning she went back to the palace and gave the king the basket. He frowned as he took out the arm. "This is too solid to be a ghost's arm."

"Ghosts can eat; and to eat, a ghost must be solid," Shell said simply. "And my picnics are worth eating."

She had no sooner spoken than the arm leapt out of the king's hand and slithered across the doorway and out to the hill. And though the king called to his soldiers to stop it, none of them dared to touch it.

"What is your final request?" Shell asked.

The king wanted her all the more. He thought and thought. "I've got you this time," he said. "I want luck. I want luck by the bushel."

And the king sat back, satisfied. If she didn't bring back his bushel of luck, then she would be his. But if she did bring him a bushel of luck, then he would conquer an empire!

That evening Shell returned to the palace with a black dog as large as a pony.

The king had Uncle Wu brought up from the dungeon under guard. When the king saw the dog, he scowled and shaped a large basket with his hands. "I wanted luck by the bushel, not a pet."

"Feed it some fire and you'll have luck by the bushel." And she gave the dog to the king. "This is the third wonder. Now free my husband."

"I only promised not to kill him," the greedy king said. "I'd be a fool to lose a treasure like you." And he ordered his soldiers to seize her.

Then he commanded Uncle Wu to bring the dog a burning log in an urn. The dog wolfed it down as if the log were a chunk of meat and looked for more, so Uncle Wu fed it a second log and then a third.

Suddenly the dog coughed and spat out a tiny flame. It shot like an arrow and landed right at the king's feet.

Leaping upon the dog's back, Shell held out her hand and helped Uncle Wu hop up behind her. Then the dog raced out through the gates and back to their home.

But all that was left of the cruel king were lumps of melted silver and burnt amber and cracked crystal and ashes.